For
Rosie
—M.B.

For those
who believe
—R.A.

Ω

Published by
Peeachtree Publishers
1700 Chattahoochee Avenue
Atlanta, GA 30318
www.peachtree-online.com

First United States edition published in 2009 by Peachtree Publishers
First published in Great Britain by Puffin Books in 2008

Artwork created in pen and ink, watercolor, pencil crayon, and collage

Printed and bound in China
10 9 8 7 6 5 4 3 2 1
First Edition

Library of Congress Cataloging-in-Publication Data

Burgess, Mark.
  Where teddy bears come from / written by Mark Burgess ; illustrated by Russell Ayto. -- 1st ed.
      p. cm.
  Summary: When Little Wolf cannot fall asleep, he decides that he needs a teddy bear and goes into the woods to see if he can find out where to get one.
  ISBN 978-1-56145-487-7 / 1-56145-487-7
  [1. Wolves--Fiction. 2. Characters in literature--Fiction. 3. Teddy bears--Fiction.] I. Ayto, Russell, ill. II. Title.
  PZ7.B91654Wh 2009
  [E]--dc22
                                                    2008052705

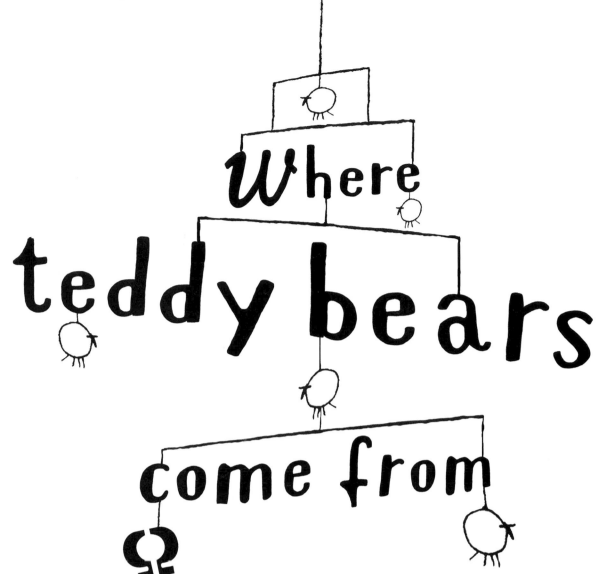

Where teddy bears come from

Written by
Mark Burgess

Illustrated by
Russell Ayto

Ω

PEACHTREE
ATLANTA

In the middle of
a deep, dark forest,
all the creatures were fast asleep
except for a little gray wolf,
who tossed and turned
and couldn't sleep a wink.

Mother Wolf
gave him a
glass of milk
and a cuddle.

Then she tucked him in
and read his favorite
teddy bear story
three times in a row.

But it was no good.

The little wolf stayed

wide awake...

In the morning, the sun streamed in his window
and shone on a picture in his book.

"That's what I need!" cried the little wolf.

"A teddy bear! That will help me sleep!"

"Where do teddy bears come from?" the little wolf
asked his mother.

But Mother Wolf didn't know. "Why don't you ask Wise Owl?"
she said. "Wise Owl knows everything."

"Yes, I will," said the little wolf bravely. Though he was rather shy,
he really wanted a teddy bear.

Mother Wolf packed a picnic for him. "Be careful," she said. "And be back by bedtime." So, the little wolf set off through the forest to find Wise Owl.

Wise Owl
was fast asleep.

"Please," whispered the little wolf.
"Where do teddy bears come from?
I can't sleep and I need a teddy bear."

Wise Owl opened one eye. "Hmm," he muttered.
"I usually have no trouble sleeping."
He opened the other eye.
"I don't know much about bears, especially teddy bears.
Perhaps you should ask the Three Little Pigs."

So the little wolf thanked him and set off through the forest.

After a while, the little wolf
came to a small brick house
beside a stream.

"The **Three Little Pigs**
must live here," said the little wolf.
"If I ask politely, perhaps they
will tell me about teddy bears."

But as the shy little wolf
approached the house,
his nose began to *twitch*,

and **tickle**,

until. . .

"A . . . A

Three **not-so-little** pigs ran out of the cottage.

"Why, if it isn't a wolf!" cried the first pig.
"Shoo, you big bad wolf, shoo!"
shouted the second pig.
"Go back to the forest right now!"
yelled the third pig.

"NO, NO, NO!" cried the little wolf.

"I'm not the **big bad wolf!**"

The three not-so-little pigs peered down at him.
"Well, if you're not the **big bad wolf,**" the first
one said, "and you don't want to **huff** and **puff**
and **blow our house down**, what *do* you want?"

"**Please,**" said the little wolf.
"**Where do teddy bears come from?**
I can't sleep and I need a teddy bear."

"Oh!" said the third pig. "Well, we don't know anything about teddy bears.
We sing lullabies to each other so we can get to sleep."
The other not-so-little pigs nodded in agreement.
"Perhaps you should ask Little Red Riding Hood."

So the little wolf thanked them and went on through the forest.

After a while, the little wolf
came to a pretty thatched cottage.

"This cottage looks very friendly,"
the little wolf said to himself.
"This time I will be brave and knock.
I'm sure **Little Red Riding Hood**
knows all about teddy bears."

The little wolf hurried up
to the front door, but his claws
were rather long and he

tripped over the

doormat…

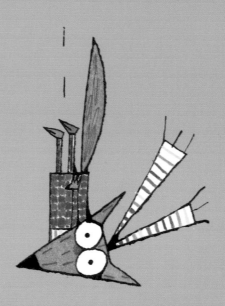

CRASH!

He
landed
in the
laundry
basket.

A girl in a scarlet cloak ran into the hallway, followed by an older woman.

"Why, if it isn't a wolf!" the girl cried. "Shoo, you big bad wolf! Shoo! Go back to the forest this very minute!"

"NO, NO, NO!" cried the little wolf. "I'm not the big bad wolf."

"Well," said the little girl crossly, "if you're not the big bad wolf and you don't want to gobble us up, what *do* you want?"

"Please," said the little wolf. "Where do teddy bears come from? I can't sleep and I need a teddy bear."

"Oh!" said the girl. "Well, we don't bother with teddy bears. We count sheep to get to sleep." Her grandma nodded in agreement. "Perhaps you should ask Goldilocks. She knows about bears."

So the little wolf thanked them and went on through the forest.

By now, the little wolf was very tired.
He wandered along, not looking where he was going,
which was how he bumped into an old man who
was bending down beside a big red truck.

"Why, if it isn't a wolf!"
cried the rosy-faced old man.

The little wolf scrambled to his feet.

"But I'm not the
big bad wolf!" he cried.

"Well, *that* is a shame,"
said the old man, "because
I need someone who can huff and
puff and blow this tire up."

"Oh, well, in that case I could
give it a try," said the little wolf.

So he huffed. . .

And he
puffed...

And he huffed
and he puffed
and he blew the tire up...
and up...

"STOP!!" cried the old man.
"That will do nicely, thank you.
Now then, little wolf, one good turn
deserves another. What can I do for you?"

"Please," said the little wolf.
"Where do teddy bears
come from?
I can't sleep and I need a teddy bear."

The old man nodded.
"HO, HO, HO!" he said.
"Where do teddy bears come from?
What a question!
If you run home right now, I promise that
you'll have the answer in the morning."

"Oh, thank you!" cried the little wolf,
and he ran all the way home.

That night, the little wolf didn't need a **glass of milk** or a **story** or a **cuddle**.

He was so tired that he fell fast asleep at once and slept the whole night through.

When he woke up the next morning there was an odd-shaped package at the foot of his bed.

"TO MY FRIEND, THE LITTLE WOLF, WITH THANKS FOR HELPING ME. XX"

The little wolf could hardly believe his eyes.

Inside the package was the softest, cuddliest teddy bear anyone could wish for. The little wolf hugged his teddy tightly and quickly ran outside.

"Now I know where
teddy bears
come from!" he cried.

From then on, the little wolf had no trouble sleeping.

And that might not be where all teddy bears come from,
but it's where this little wolf got his.